The Plea

PRAISE FOR *STORYSHARES*

"One of the brightest innovators and game-changers in the education industry."
– Forbes

"Your success in applying research-validated practices to promote literacy serves as a valuable model for other organizations seeking to create evidence-based literacy programs."

- Library of Congress

"We need powerful social and educational innovation, and Storyshares is breaking new ground. The organization addresses critical problems facing our students and teachers. I am excited about the strategies it brings to the collective work of making sure every student has an equal chance in life."
– Teach For America

"Around the world, this is one of the up-and-coming trailblazers changing the landscape of literacy and education."
- International Literacy Association

"It's the perfect idea. There's really nothing like this. I mean wow, this will be a wonderful experience for young people."   - Andrea Davis Pinkney, Executive Director, Scholastic

"Reading for meaning opens opportunities for a lifetime of learning. Providing emerging readers with engaging texts that are designed to offer both challenges and support for each individual will improve their lives for years to come. Storyshares is a wonderful start."
- David Rose, Co-founder of CAST & UDL

The Plea

Kaitlyn O'Malley

STORYSHARES

Story Share, Inc.
New York. Boston. Philadelphia

Published in the United States by Story Share, Inc.

Storyshares
Story Share, Inc.
24 N. Bryn Mawr Avenue #340
Bryn Mawr, PA 19010-3304
www.storyshares.org

Inspiring reading with a new kind of book.

Interest Level: High School
Grade Level Equivalent: 5.2

9781642612028

Book design by Storyshares

Printed in the United States of America

Storyshares Presents

1

They say that Allah is forgiving and that you should forgive a person as often as you would wish for Allah to forgive you. I have often prided myself on my dedication to my belief. I have prided myself on the fact that when the Day of Judgment comes, I will be reunited with Him. So perhaps He will be willing to forgive me for my inability to forgive others.

It's not that I haven't tried. I have. In fact, I used to stay up late at night praying that my forgiveness would stop all tragedy. But Asif has never taken well to the influence of others.

The attacks were on the news yesterday. Asif was too, under a fake name, of course. But I would recognize his face anywhere, even after twelve years. He had the same dark brown eyes, still glazed with mystery and a hint of amusement. There was still a faint scar on the crook of his nose from when he had run into a post while playing in the schoolyard as a child.

I could see the beginnings of a grin forming on his face, even behind his newly grown beard. Only I would notice these things. Despite the fact that they are asking people to call and identify the suspect, I won't. I suppose that makes me a liar, but I hope Allah forgives me for that too.

This morning when I woke up, I heard about the bombings in Karbala on the news. Hundreds died, victims to the merciless gunfire of the extremist group. They didn't air footage of any of the bodies. They never do. That way, the horror of it all doesn't seem so real. Only landscape images of Iraqi deserts and central Karbala city streets flashed across the screen. Pre-recorded videos of masked gunmen were occasionally broadcast.

Karbala was the sixth in a string of terrorist attacks executed by Asif and his Sunni extremist group on Shiite Iraqi cities. According to the reporters, they had driven through the city in an armed vehicle, shooting anyone who dared to get in their way. The news made him sound like a villain, but then again, you can't trust the media to deliver the truth.

I turned off the television. They were beginning to mention specific details about the attacks. I couldn't bear to hear. There comes a point when your mind chooses to block out reality because it has become too real, and you would much rather be free in your own spiritual fantasies.

I had been thinking of Asif a lot recently. I couldn't seem to get my mind off of him, which sounds sinful, but I was only remembering the times that we used to spend together. I thought of how close we used to be. I wouldn't describe us as "close" anymore.

It was time for Dhuhr prayer, and the sun was looking almost directly down at the scattered village of Mosul. The heat was pleasantly warm.

I had always lived on the outskirts of the city, nowhere near the bustling streets and crowded commercial centers that were a large part of Mosul. The nearest food market was a kilometer away. You would have to walk several more kilometers before you could see any sort of large-scale building or corporation.

I didn't mind the journey. It provided me more time to connect with Allah. It became a way for me to pray to Him outside of the times when millions of others did. Perhaps then He would be more attentive to my prayers.

The village had stayed the same over the years. I had been living there since I was born twenty-seven years ago. The layout and population remained stable, so I had almost gotten used to the monotonous lifestyle. Almost.

There was one big change that prevented anyone from getting used to it: the safety. All around Mosul, groups of armed officers patrolled the borders, making sure the city was secure and that there was no suspicious activity in the area. That was never an issue when I was a child, but then again, that was when Asif was a child, too.

2

"Huda!" I heard a soft voice call from outside, accompanied by the sound of a fist banging against my door. I walked into the foyer and waited for Abba to check who was at the door. I, of course, knew who it was, but it was custom for him to open the door first.

Abba swung open the door, revealing a boy dressed in a dirtied thobe, with short, black hair and dark brown eyes.

"Salaam, Asif." Abba smiled, opening the door wider.

"Salaam, sir," Asif, who was about nine at the time, returned the greeting. "Can Huda come out and play?"

Abba nodded, stepping aside from the entrance. I smiled and made sure that my scarf was wrapped tightly around my head before walking out and joining Asif.

He was always coming over to our house, asking to play. Perhaps it was because he didn't want to spend time at home. His parents never went out with him. I didn't know why.

Occasionally, he would show up at our door looking bruised and beaten but still asking to play. *Always* asking to play, never anything else. When I asked Asif about the marks once, he just shrugged it off, saying that was what would happen if I ever tried to play football. I had never known that football could leave such bruises.

It was a windy morning, and the air was plagued with a thin layer of dust that attacked our eyes so we could only see a few feet in front of us. The wind carried a wave of heat, making the weather even less enjoyable than usual.

"Perfect weather," Asif announced, a smile spreading across his face.

"What for?" I asked, noticing the excitement in his eyes.

I had been taught to say very little, as all young girls were. In fact, we were often taught to nod and say nothing at all. But Asif made that difficult. He asked questions, expecting a response in return. I could do nothing but answer. Abba would have scolded me.

"You'll see." Then he started running down the street toward central Mosul, dodging people and sprinting so fast it was as if the wind was carrying him. "Follow me!" he yelled behind him, so I did.

I don't know how many kilometers we ran through the city. I don't know how many looks people gave us as we did. All I know is that we ran until my feet were so numb that I couldn't feel the pain in my legs. We ran until I didn't recognize the surrounding buildings.

We were well into central Mosul. Gradually, the number of cars driving on the streets increased, and we had to run on the sidewalk to avoid them.

Asif began to slow down as he reached the river bank.

The Tigris River ran straight through Mosul. Its remarkably clear waters and steady currents made the river one of Mosul's, and Iraq's, major destinations.

"Asif," I called, making sure to keep my voice low so people walking by wouldn't hear me. "What are you doing?"

Our eyes met for a moment. Then Asif turned away and jumped over the barrier to the river bank. I ran over to the cement wall, searching below for Asif, hoping he hadn't already waded into the Tigris. When I didn't see him right away, horror jolted down my spine.

"Asif!" I yelled, frantic. "Asif!" I closed my eyes, trying to stay calm by muttering prayers and asking for help from Allah.

"Shhhh!" a familiar voice hissed. I saw Asif standing directly below, cleverly hidden by the ledge. "Yallah. Come on." The boy motioned me down. I looked around cautiously before hopping over the barrier.

Asif was always doing that: going off on crazy adventures and scaring me by putting himself in danger. I watched as he walked over to the river and began stepping into the water.

"What are you doing?" I exclaimed, running after him.

"It's a hot day, Huda," he informed me, as if I wasn't already aware. "We are going swimming."

"No," I stepped back, folding my arms over my chest. There was no way that I was swimming in the river. "We'll get in trouble."

"Please, Huda."

"No."

"Fine," Asif said, pursing his lips and glancing around. "Do what you want."

"Thank you."

All of a sudden, he was running up to me and grabbing me by my arms, tugging me into the river.

"Asif!" I wailed, giggling as he practically dragged me backward. "I said no."

But it was too late. He had already managed to pull me in. After I had gotten over the coolness of the water and managed to gather my balance with the river's gentle current, he released me.

"Fun, right?" He was smirking slightly. It was so unnatural that, right there in the Tigris River, I couldn't help but laugh.

3

As we both got older, there were days when Asif and I would do nothing adventurous. Instead we would sit and talk. Of course, he would do most of the talking. I would interject on occasion, but it was talking nonetheless. We would speak about whatever Asif wanted to speak about, whether school or Mosul or family or Allah. I never cared what the topic was as long as I got to spend more time with my friend.

"Are you free, Huda?" Asif asked after Abba opened the door one day.

"Yes." I smiled, stepping out into the street. "I am."

Asif nodded to Abba and off we went. I could tell the day would be filled with more talking than activity. Asif got a certain look on his face when he wanted to talk. I was always looking forward to a day when I got to listen to him.

As we walked, I noticed that he had a red slash across his cheek, but as always, I said nothing. Over the years I had learned that he didn't want to discuss such things.

"How are you?" he asked. He wasn't smiling, but I could see that he was trying to keep his mood light.

"Well," I replied simply. We walked in silence for several minutes. I waited for Asif to speak again. When he didn't, I decided that I should. "I suppose you're not so well."

He responded with a question. "Do you think it is true that Allah has His reasons for everything He does?" It used to frustrate me how he did that, but I had gotten used to it. Before I could respond, Asif continued, "Because I am having trouble finding the reason behind His latest decision."

"What happened, Asif?" I placed my hand gently on his shoulder, concerned, but careful not to keep it there for too long. Even though it was quite late and people were beginning to return home, we were still in public.

"Abba says we must leave Mosul," he said quietly, as if it pained him to even speak the words. "I don't know where we're going or why we're leaving, but all I know is that I don't think we are going to return."

It was then that I stopped walking, suddenly tired. A heavy and overwhelming feeling weighed me down. After the eight years that we had known each other, ever since we were six, Asif was leaving. I couldn't believe it.

"And I don't want to go, Huda," he said. "Mosul is my home."

My heart hurt. My eyes burned from the tears that I was holding back. Abba would have scolded me for how attached I had become to Asif, but I couldn't help it. However, I also knew how attached Asif had become to me. I knew that unless I convinced him otherwise, he would never be happy outside of Mosul.

"Allah does do everything for a reason," I told him, never looking directly into his eyes.

I knew that if I told him I didn't want him to go, it would only make things worse. And it is one of the teachings of Islam to make things easy for people, not difficult.

"I am sure that He has a reason for this. You must learn to accept it and learn from it. He makes no mistakes. Even our names were chosen for us. Just look at their meanings. Mine means 'right guidance.' What about yours?" I was trying to take his mind off of the news. I was also trying to take my mind off of it.

"Forgiveness," he stated simply. And for the second time that day, we stood in silence for several minutes, almost as if each of us was remembering our friendship. Neither one of us would look the other in the eye. "I will miss you, Huda."

In my mind, I kept repeating the Islamic teaching of making things easier for others. That was why, even though I wanted to, I did not say that I would miss him too.

Asif sighed, understanding that I had nothing more to say. He changed topics. We had reached the edge of the city and were standing beside the final buildings.

Ahead of us there was only desert and probably another city in the distance.

"Look," Asif said, tapping me on the shoulder and pointing out towards the desert. With my back turned away from the village, I could see nothing but desert. Of course, I had seen the sands many times before but never like this. Never when the sun was setting, the village nearly asleep, and Asif by my side. I was afraid to breathe, fearing that any noise would ruin the moment.

The view was so hypnotizing that, for a moment, I forgot Asif was beside me. I forgot everything he had said. The sun, a ball of fire, burned streaks of red and orange into the blue sky. It shone so brightly that it illuminated the sand.

The yellow sand went on forever, kissing the sky with its burning lips. The dunes were like calming ocean waves in the way they rolled into one another. It amazed me how an infinite amount of grains made up the desert. Alone, each grain of sand could represent nothing, but united, they painted an image so spectacular it could take anyone's breath away.

"Allah was an incredible artist," Asif spoke softly, his gaze never leaving the desert. I could only reply with silence, for there were no words to describe such beauty.

We were fourteen then. That was the last time I saw Asif.

4

Those memories seemed unreal because I could barely remember the person Asif used to be. I could barely remember the conversations we used to have. The last time we talked was that evening during the desert sunset.

The attacks had been getting closer to the city in recent days. I believed that as long as I stayed in Mosul I would be safe because Asif knew I was here. I believed he would never attack his own city. No, I *knew* that he wouldn't.

I wrapped my scarf around my head and prepared to make my way to the mosque for prayer. My husband and son, Samih, had already left. I had chosen to give my son that name because it meant "Forgiver." I felt that, in a way, Asif was here with me every day.

As most families did, we attended separate mosques, so I always left after them. There was something about solitude that gave me time to think deeply about my life, and, on occasion, about Asif.

One of the hadiths in the Qur'an says that if you follow up a bad deed with a good one, you can cancel it out. I doubted that Asif would change his ways now that he was so invested. But, for a moment, I considered the idea that maybe the hadith worked if it was reversed. If you followed up a *good* deed with a *bad* one, would the good deed become meaningless?

My thoughts were interrupted by a sudden burst of screams from outside. I rushed to the door to see crowds of people and families running from central Mosul. Mothers clutched their children and ran behind their husbands. Looks of horror and fear were plastered across their faces.

"Yallah! Come quickly!" one of the patrolling guards shouted over the panicked crowds, ushering people out of the city. "We have to leave, now!"

"Huda!" In the distance, I saw my husband running towards our small house, Samih in his arms. "We must leave. There was a bomb threat. Quickly, follow me!"

Frantically, he grabbed my arm, and we began swimming through the crowd, heading toward the desert. I clutched my husband's arm, making sure not to lose him in the chaos. My heart was filled with terror and concern for both myself and my family. Asif was always doing that, going off on crazy adventures and scaring me.

The Plea

20

About The Author

Kaitlyn O'Malley is a contributing author to the Storyshares library.

About The Publisher

Story Shares is a nonprofit focused on supporting the millions of teens and adults who struggle with reading by creating a new shelf in the library specifically for them. The ever-growing collection features content that is compelling and culturally relevant for teens and adults, yet still readable at a range of lower reading levels.

Story Shares generates content by engaging deeply with writers, bringing together a community to create this new kind of book. With more intriguing and approachable stories to choose from, the teens and adults who have fallen behind are improving their skills and beginning to discover the joy of reading. For more information, visit storyshares.org.

Easy to Read. Hard to Put Down.

www.ingramcontent.com/pod-product-compliance
Lightning Source LLC
Chambersburg PA
CBHW071230170626
46809CB00005BA/2019